# A WISH FOR ELVES

MARK GONYEA

Henry Holt and Company ▲ New York

Henry Holt and Company, LLC
*Publishers since 1866*
175 Fifth Avenue
New York, New York 10010
www.HenryHoltKids.com

Library of Congress Cataloging-in-Publication Data
Gonyea, Mark.
A wish for elves / Mark Gonyea. — 1st ed.
p.    cm.
Summary: A boy makes a wish for a little holiday help, and while he gets more
than he bargained for, Santa pays the price.
ISBN 978-0-8050-8814-4
[1. Elves—Fiction.  2. Santa Claus—Fiction.  3. Christmas—Fiction.]  I. Title.
PZ7.G5874Wis 2010    [E]—dc22    2009030624

First Edition—2010
Printed in May 2010 in China by Macmillan Production (Asia) Ltd., Kwun Tong,
Kowloon, Hong Kong (Supplier Code: 10), on acid-free paper. ∞

1 3 5 7 9 10 8 6 4 2

**DEDICATED TO MOM, DAD, MIKE, JENN, & ABBY**

LIFE WOULD BE EASIER...

...IF I HAD ELVES TOO!

HAVE YOU
SEEN US?

HI THERE!

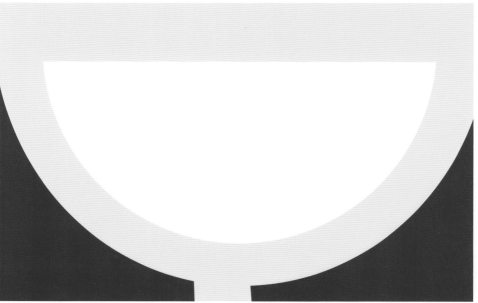